T
AN

The little red bus has trouble getting its passengers to town because of the snow, while Polly is made a hat by her friends so that she can go to tea with the Queen, and Mrs Bly finally finds some plums to make her plum pie. These are just three of the six rhyming stories brought together in this book. Taken from six books originally published individually in the 1960s, this collection will delight all children today with its jolly characters, lively rhythms and rhymes, and enchanting illustrations.

Miss Read is perhaps best known as the creator of the *Thrush Green* and *Village School* books and she has written in total over forty books for adults. Miss Read now lives and works with her husband in their country cottage in Berkshire.

THE
LITTLE
RED BUS

AND OTHER RHYMING STORIES

MISS READ

ILLUSTRATIONS BY
JONATHAN LANGLEY

PUFFIN BOOKS

PUFFIN BOOKS

Published by the Penguin Group
Penguin Books Ltd, 27 Wrights Lane, London W8 5TZ, England
Penguin Books USA Inc., 375 Hudson Street, New York, New York 10014, USA
Penguin Books Australia Ltd, Ringwood, Victoria, Australia
Penguin Books Canada Ltd, 10 Alcorn Avenue, Toronto, Ontario, Canada M4V 3B2
Penguin Books (NZ) Ltd, 182–190 Wairau Road, Auckland 10, New Zealand

Penguin Books Ltd, Registered Offices: Harmondsworth, Middlesex, England

First published by Viking 1991
Published in Puffin Books 1993
3 5 7 9 10 8 6 4 2

Text copyright © 'Miss Read' and Thomas Nelson and Sons Ltd, 1964
Illustrations copyright © Jonathan Langley, 1991
All rights reserved

The moral right of the author and illustrator has been asserted

Printed in England by Clays Ltd, St Ives plc
Filmset in Times (Linotron 202)

Contents

The
Little
Red Bus

This is a bus.
It is shiny and red.
It stands every night
In this very big shed.

Now this man is Fred.
He comes every day
To drive the red bus
To town far away.

Now one night, when Fred
Was lying in bed,
And the shiny red bus
Was at rest in the shed,

THE SNOW CAME – so fast
That, by the next day,
Poor Fred had to dig
To his bus, all the way.

He got in his bus
And he said: "We must go
To town with the people –
Snow or no snow!

Up over the hill
And then we run down.
The people are waiting
To go into town!"

But the shiny red bus
Found the hill very steep,
And it could not go on
For the snow was too deep.

"Let's give you a push
Up this steep hill," said Fred,
And he pushed and he pushed
Till his face was quite red.

But the shiny red bus
Was stuck fast in the snow
On the side of the hill –
And it just could not go.

The people were waiting
Not far away.
"Now where is the bus?
We shall be late today!"

"I must do my shopping,"
Said fat Mrs Bly,
"I want fish for my cat
And some plums for a pie."

"And we want plums too,"
Said Betty to Pat.
"And ribbon," said Polly,
"To trim my best hat."

But the shiny red bus
Was still stuck in the snow
On the side of the hill –
And it just could not go.

Just then came a postman.
"Can I help?" he said,
So the two pushed and pushed
Till their faces were red.

But the shiny red bus
Was still stuck in the snow
On the side of the hill –
And it just could not go.

And then came a farmer.
"Can I help?" he said,
So the three pushed and pushed
Till their faces were red.

But the shiny red bus
Was still stuck in the snow
On the side of the hill –
And it just could not go.

And then came a milkman.
"Can I help?" he said,
So the four pushed and pushed
Till their faces were red.

But the shiny red bus
Was still stuck in the snow
On the side of the hill –
And it just could not go.

The milkman, the farmer,
The postman and Fred,
All looked at the bus
In its deep snowy bed.

"We must have more help,"
Said the milkman,
            "I KNOW!
My horse could help pull
This bus out of the snow!"

They tied the good horse
To the bus with a rope.
"You pull while we push,
And we'll shift it, we hope."

The milkman, the farmer,
The postman and Fred,
All pushed at the back
Till their faces were red.

And the horse pulled in front,
With a puff and a blow –
And the bus slowly came
From its bed in the snow.

They pushed and they pulled
To the top of the hill.
"Well done, horse!" they said,
When at last he stood still.

They gave him a pat.
"Without him, I know,"
Said Fred, "my red bus
Would still be in the snow."

Fred got in his bus.
"Thank you, friends," he called down,
And they all waved goodbye
As he drove off to town.

"Hooray! Here it comes!
There's the bus! And there's Fred!
We *can* go to town
After all!" people said.

"I'm sorry I'm late,"
Said Fred, "but you see
We have had an adventure,
My red bus and me."

And he told them about
The steep hill and the snow,
And the friends who had helped
When the bus could not go.

And you can be sure
That he told them –
OF COURSE –
Of the friend who helped most –
The milkman's good horse.

Cluck,
the Little
Black Hen

Here is Cluck,
A little black hen.

Here is her master.
His name is Ben.

Every morning
At half past ten,
Cluck lays an egg
For her master Ben.

Sometimes she lays
Her egg in the shed,
Where the golden straw
Makes a soft dry bed.

Sometimes she lays
Her egg in the hay.
The haystack is warm
On a windy day.

Sometimes she lays
Her egg in a spot
That is cool and green,
When the sun is hot.

And when it's laid
She clucks with glee:
"I've laid an egg!
Come, Ben, and see!"

So every morning
At half past ten,
A game begins
For Master Ben.

He looks for his egg.
He looks in the shed
Where the golden straw
Makes a soft dry bed.

He looks for his egg.
He looks in the hay.
He says: "Where is
My egg today?"

He looks everywhere.
"Now little black hen,
Where have you hidden
My egg?" says Ben.

And little black hen
She clucks with glee:
"Just look, Master Ben,
Just look and see!"

But one fine day
When the sun is hot,
Cluck lays her egg
In a secret spot.

Ben looks here
And Ben looks there,
But he can't find it
Anywhere.

He looks everywhere.
"Now, little black hen,
Where have you hidden
My egg?" says Ben.

But little black hen
Just looks away.
"I'm not telling YOU!"
She seems to say.

The very next day
When the sun is hot,
Cluck lays one more
In the secret spot.

And every day,
In rain or shine,
She lays one more –
Till there are nine.

The secret spot
Is cool and green.
"I'll sit very still
And I won't be seen.

I'm quite safe here!"
Says little black hen.
"I'll hide all my eggs
From my master Ben."

For three weeks Ben
Looks here and there,
But he can't find Cluck
Anywhere.

"She must be lost,
My lovely hen!
I can't think where
She is!" says Ben.

"No game of hide
And seek to play
With Cluck, at
Half past ten each day!

I miss her so.
Where can she be?
I WISH she would
Come back to me!"

And then he listens.
Can he hear
The sound of clucking
Very near?

And is that something
Soft and black?
"Why, Cluck!" says Ben,
"At last you're back!"

Then Cluck comes strutting,
Proud and slow,
With nine baby chicks
In one long row.

"Now you can see,"
She seems to say,
"Why THIS game took
So long to play!"

"You clever Cluck!
Hooray!" says Ben.
"I had one hen –
And now I've TEN!"

Plum
Pie

This is
Mrs Bly.
One day she said:
"I'll make –
A plum pie!"

She put on her coat,
She put on her hat,
She put on her gloves,
And –

She put out the cat.

She ran to the shops
In the wink of an eye,
And all she could think of
Was sizzling plum pie.

The man in the fruit shop said:
"Well, Mrs Bly,
Is there anything here
That you'd like to try?

I have all sorts of fruit
In my shop, as you see –"
Said fat Mrs Bly:
"Just plums, please, for me."

"There are no plums
I'm sorry to say,
No plums at all
In the shop today."

"NO PLUMS FOR MY PIE?
In a fruit shop too!
NO PLUMS AT ALL?
But what can I do?"

"Well, what about apples?
They make a fine pie.
I'm sure you would like them
If only you'd try."

"I don't want apples,
I don't, I say.
It's plums I want –
Just plums today!"

"Well, what about oranges,
Juicy and sweet?
I'm sure you would like
A sweet orange to eat."

"I don't want oranges,
I don't, that's that!
It's plums I want
JUST PLUMS!
          That's flat!"

"But we have no plums
In the shop today!
No plums at all
I'm sorry to say!"

"I just want plums,"
Said fat Mrs Bly.
"I just want plums
For a fine plum pie.

You call this a fruit shop!
And you stand there
And tell me NO PLUMS!
I shall go elsewhere!"

So fat Mrs Bly
Ran back down the street,
Wondering where there were
Plums to eat.

"There are no more fruit shops,"
Said poor Mrs Bly.
She took out her hanky
And started to cry.

"I shall never," she sobbed,
"Make that sizzling plum pie."

She sobbed and she mopped
As she sat on a wall
And she mopped and sobbed:
"No pie after all."

Just then someone said:
"Oh, poor Mrs Bly!
Why are you sobbing?
And why do you cry?"

"I'm glad to tell someone,"
Said damp Mrs Bly,
And she told him she longed
For a sizzling plum pie.

"But it's never to be,"
Said poor Mrs Bly,
"For there isn't a plum to be had
For my pie."

"No plums! Oh, what nonsense!
NO PLUMS? Come with me.
At the end of my garden
I have a plum tree.
I'll show you some plums,
Mrs Bly! Come and see!"

The good man was right.
"My goodness! Oh my!
There must be a million!"
Said fat Mrs Bly.

She filled up her basket,
Her eyes were soon dry.
"You are a good friend,"
Said fat Mrs Bly.
"I will call in tomorrow
And bring a plum pie!"

She ran down the street
In the wink of an eye,
And all she could think of
Was sizzling plum pie.

She took off her coat,
She took off her hat,
She took off her gloves,

And –
She took in the cat.

And she did have plum pie
After all –

And that's that!

The
Little Peg
Doll

Here is a peg
And here is May,
Who made it into
A doll one day.

She made a face,
A hat and frock,
And stood the doll
Beside the clock.

May's other dolls
Began to stare
And whispered: "Who
Is that doll there?"

"How small she is!"
Said Mary Jane,
"Yes, much too small
And much too plain."

"How small she is!"
Said Teddy Bear,
"No bigger than
The clock up there."

"How small she is!"
Said Scottish Meg,
"She's just a small
Plain wooden peg."

Then all the dolls
Began to say:
"It really isn't
Fair of May.

Just look! No bigger
Than the clock!
And what a horrid
Paper frock!

She's just a peg.
She's much too small.
She's really not
A doll at all!"

They turned their heads
The other way.
"It really isn't
Fair of May!"

But little Peg Doll
In her paper frock
Stood proud and still
Beside the clock.
She knew that she
Was small and plain –
Not big and grand
Like Mary Jane.

She knew that she
Was just a peg,
And not as fine
As Scottish Meg.

But May had made her
And her frock –
So Peg stood proudly
By the clock.

One day a parcel
Came for May.
It said: With love
From Uncle Ray.

"How big it is!
What can it be?"
May took the paper off
To see.

There stood a doll's house
Big and fine.
"Just think!" said May,
"This house is mine!"

The dolls were just
As pleased as May.
"A house for dolls,"
They said. "Hooray!"

Said Mary Jane:
"What fun to see
A house made specially
For me!"

Said Teddy Bear:
"What fun to see
A house made specially
For me!"

Said Scottish Meg:
"What fun to see
A house made specially
For me!"

Inside they saw
A table, chairs,
A bath, a bed,
And lots of stairs.

A fire, a lamp,
A book to read –
Just everything
A doll could need.

Peg Doll could only
Stand and stare
At all the lovely things
In there.

She longed to go
And try the chairs,
And poke the fire,
And climb the stairs,
And light the lamp,
And read the book –
But she could only
Stand and look.

"Come, Mary Jane,"
Said May, "and see
What Uncle Ray
Has given me.

You can't get in,
You are too wide,
But look at all
The things inside.

Your foot is bigger
Than this chair.
You are too big
To fit in there.

Come, Teddy Bear,"
Said May, "and see
What Uncle Ray
Has given me.

You can't get in,
You are too wide,
But look at all
The things inside.

This bath makes you
A little hat.
You are too big
To sit in that.

Come, Scottish Meg,"
Said May, "and see
What Uncle Ray
Has given me.

You can't get in,
You are too wide,
But look at all
The things inside.

You see this table's
Much too small.
Poor Meg, you are
Too big and tall.

You're all too big,
You're all too wide,
You're all too tall
To get inside!"

Said May: "Come,
Little Peg Doll dear,
I think that you
Will fit in here.

The chairs are right,
The table too,
Why, everything's
The size for you!

You look just right,
Peg Doll," said May,
"This house is your house
From today."

Peg Doll could only
Stand and stare.
To think that she
Should live in there!

Now she could use
The bath, the chairs,
The fire, the lamp,
The book, the stairs.

Said Peg: "I'm glad
I am so small,
For I'm the luckiest
Doll of all!"

No
Hat!

Here is a hat

And here is a hat

One hat is Betty's
And one hat is Pat's.

But look!
Here is Polly,
And she has
NO HAT.

"No hat!" says Betty.
"No hat!" says Pat.
"Polly, you can't
Go about like that!"

"No hat for me.
For I like the fun
Of shaking my hair
In the wind and the sun!"

"You may like to feel
The wind and the sun,

But to go in the rain
With no hat
Is no fun."

"No hat for Polly!
I say it again
No hat in the wind
Or the sun or the rain.
No! No hat for Polly!
NO HAT!
Is that plain?"

One morning a letter
Is flat on the mat.
Look, it says: "Betty
And Polly and Pat,"
And look, here's a crown.
But what can this mean?

Betty and Polly and Pat
— o —
The Queen has a Party
And hopes that all three
Can come to the Garden
Today and take tea.

Please wear a hat

Says Betty: "This letter
Has come from
THE QUEEN!"

Tea with the Queen!
But look, what is that?
Here at the end it says:

PLEASE WEAR A HAT

"Look, Polly," says Betty,
"Look, Polly," says Pat.
"For tea with the Queen,
You MUST wear a hat."

"There's no time to buy one
We'll make one instead,
With flowers from the garden
And straw from the shed."

They sit in the garden.
All three of them plait
The straw from the shed
For Polly's new hat.

It takes all the morning
To make a long plait.
"There's no time for dinner,"
Says Polly to Pat,
"For look at the clock,
It says it is one
And there's sewing to do
Before my hat's done."

They start at the crown
Of the hat.
It is fun
To see the hat grow
From the plait they have done.

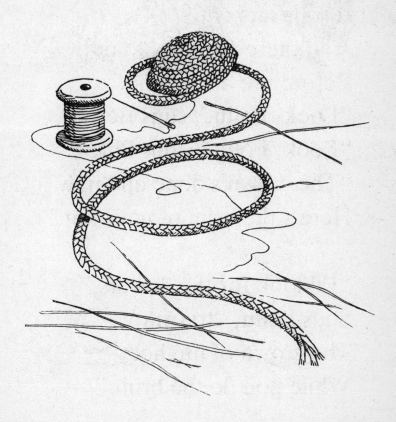

"Look, Polly," says Betty,
"Look, Polly," says Pat.
"The crown's done and now
Here's the brim of your hat."

"I'll look for the flowers,"
Says Polly, "to trim
The crown of my hat
While you do the brim."

"Look, poppies and daisies,
Red, white and green,
To make a plain hat
Fine enough for the Queen."

And now it is done,
"It's a love of a hat
And you look simply fine!"
Say Betty and Pat.

"You've made it so well,"
Says Polly, "that's why.
But look at the clock!
It says three. We must fly."

By four they are tidy
And clean for the Queen.
They go to the party
In red, white and green.

Says Polly: "The rain
And the wind and the sun
Are all very well –
But a hat can be fun!"

And Pat looks at Betty,
And Betty at Pat –
At last Polly's tidy,
AND PLEASED with a HAT!

The Queen wears her crown.
She bows to the three,
As they curtsy, and says to them:
"Do have some tea."

She looks very kindly
At Betty and Pat,
But to Polly she says:
"What a LOVE of a hat!

It's the prettiest here!"
Says the Queen.

And that's that.

The
New Bed

Here is a boy,
His name is Ted.
Here is the cot
Which is his bed.

The side was up
When he was small,
To make quite sure
He did not fall.

But now it can
Stay down, as Ted
Is quite safe when
He goes to bed.

Sometimes Ted pulls
It up to be
A sailor, or
A ship at sea.

Sometimes he roars
And rumbles too,
Just like a lion
At the Zoo.

Sometimes he turns
Into a clown,
And jumps and bumps
High up and down.

But when he can't
Play any more,
He puts the side
Down as before,

And counts the beads,
Some blue, some white,
Before he falls
Asleep each night.

One two three
Four five – and then –
Six seven eight and
Nine and ten.

One day his mother
Says to Ted:
"Just come and see
Your fine new bed."

"New bed?" says Ted,
"I don't want one.
I like my cot.
It's much more fun."

"But Ted, your cot
Is much too small.
You are too big,
You are too tall –
It's time you had
A grown-up bed."

"I'd rather have
My cot!" says Ted.

"I like the sides,
So I can be
A sailor, or
A ship at sea.

I like to roar
And rumble too,
Just like a lion
At the Zoo.

I like to turn
Into a clown
And jump and bump
High up and down.

I like to count
My beads each night.
A bed with no beads
Won't be right.

I like to count
One two three four
Five six seven eight –
And then two more."

But mother takes
The cot, and Ted
Sleeps in his grown-up
Bed instead.

"This bed is big
And fine – but NOT –"
Says Ted, "a PATCH
On my old cot!

I wish I had
My beads," says Ted.
"I'll count my fingers
Here instead.

One two and three
Four five – and then –
Six seven and eight
And nine and ten.

You see? A fellow
Only needs
Two hands if he
Has lost his beads.

One two three four,
I'll count again.
Five six and seven
Eight nine and ten.

I think I'll grow
To like this bed,
Although there are
No beads," says Ted.

"For beads are fine
When you are small,
But they're for BABIES
After all!"

So Ted sleeps soundly
Every night
In his new bed
Of blue and white,
And quite forgets
The cot where he
Once played, and counted
One two three –

Till one day Father
Comes to Ted,
And says: "Jump quickly
Out of bed.

There's something new
For you to see.
It's in our room.
Just come with me."

There, in Ted's cot
Of blue and white,
A baby sleeps
All tucked up tight.

Says Father: "There
Is your new brother."
"What do you think
Of him?" says Mother.

"Hooray!" says Ted
And hugs his mother.
"I hoped I'd get
A baby brother.

I'll show him how
To sail and roar,
And jump and bump,
And what is more –

I'll teach him how
To count to ten –
And we can use
The beads again!

And when he's big
As me," says Ted,
"I'll let him sleep
In my new bed!"